Backwoods

By

Taylor Ann Stone

Table of Contents

Chapter 1

"Alright campers! Get on the bus, get comfy, and get ready for the next two weeks of your life in the woods!" A voice rings out above the general chatter of all the teenagers. The talking fades out for a moment while everyone listens to him but the moment he's done talking, everyone seems to be complaining at once.

It's not a very friendly environment. I'm standing near the back of the crowd, trying to stay away and maybe plotting an escape. Standing in the middle of a parking lot with dozens of random teenagers is maybe the most hostile environment for me to be in.

And unfortunately, there's really no escape. Summer camp is going to be my reality for the next two weeks and there's nothing I can do about it. I watch with a rising feeling of anxiety in my stomach as a school bus pulls up in front of the crowd and people start to pile in.

I'm one of the last people on and immediately I find myself utterly lost. People have paired up, filling up seats. People are swinging their backpacks, talking to each other, moving around. The entire bus seems to be full until I make it to the very back. There are a few empty seats and I barely make it to an empty seat before my legs give out and I collapse.

I can't do this. I can't do this. I think to myself. I don't know a single person on this bus and already I can tell what type of people these are. I recognized a few faces as I walked to the back of the bus, mostly popular kids and school bullies being forced into summer camp by their parents in summer camp will fix their garbage attitudes.

And I'm the one they pick on at school. I've been able to hide from them for the last two school years, but now they'll be the people I have to interact with every day. Just the thought of it is enough to make me start to feel nauseous before someone sits on the seat next to me.

"Hey! I'm Annie, who are you?" She says brightly. I stare at her for a moment, trying to get a grasp on reality again.

She must be around my age since the camp is only open to high schoolers but she looks so young. Her eyes are bright and curious. Her curly brown hair is pulled back into a puffy ponytail with wisps of curls framing her face. Her bright clothing is in stark contrast against her brown skin and she looks... dorky.

"Connor. It's nice to meet you." I finally say, trying not to be rude. She doesn't seem to mind at all, and shrugs off her backpack and places it on the floor, in between her legs. I've never seen her around at school, but at the same time, she seems the type that would've been bullied. She must just be good at hiding.

Like me.

"It's nice to meet you too. We can be friends if you want." She says, smiling at me. I feel my anxiety lift a little bit and even though it's a bit childish, I find myself nodding. More than anything, right now, I want a friend.

"Oh, yeah. Yeah, that would be great." I find myself smiling back at her. I don't know why but I have a good feeling about her. Maybe this summer camp thing won't be so bad.

"Is this your first year attending?"

Even though she dresses a bit weird and she looks a little young, she seems to be completely relaxed in the chaos of the bus. People are still moving around and shouting, but at the back of the bus, it's quiet enough that we can just talk normally to each other.

"Yeah. This is my first time."

"Well, it isn't that bad. I promise." Annie says. I find myself believing her words as I study her face. Her expression lights up as someone else sits at the seat in front of us. "And this is Jonathon!"

I glance up and I have to double-take. He's an older boy, with curly brown hair that's pulled back into a small ponytail. He's one of the taller boys, athletic, and he's got sharp features that make him look intense.

Oh. And I… I recognize that face. He's a senior at my school, we have a few classes together. Both because he's been held back and because I'm in accelerated classes.

My heart starts to pick up speed again and the anxious twist in my stomach is back full force. But Annie doesn't seem to notice at all.

"You can call me Jonny. Hey Annie." Jonny says, giving me a wave. My brain freezes for a moment before I nod back to him.

I don't understand why he's sitting here with us. From what I remember in school, he was somewhat popular and he would probably fit in fine with the louder bullies and populars at the front of the bus. Still, Annie seems to know him.

"This is Connor. He's new." Annie gestures at me. Jonny stares at me for a moment and I freeze up again. Does he remember me from the few classes we've had together? Does he know all the rumors about me? Is he disgusted?

"Oh, yeah don't stress about all of this. Kids can be really big assholes, but if you just want to chill with me and Annie, that's fine." Jonny waves at the group of people at the front of the bus. He's got a low, relaxed voice that sends shivers up my spine. His grey eyes lock on me and I have the feeling that he's studying me.

"Yeah… That sounds good." I breathe. He finally nods and he drops his gaze, turning to face the front of the bus. He places his backpack on the seat next to him, lying down across the seat and stretching out. I catch a glimpse of his stomach as he stretches his arms above his head and I stare at the hint of his happy trail and boxers peeking above his jeans.

"Good. Now, he's going to nap for the next two hours." Annie says.

Maybe summer camp won't be so bad.

Chapter 2

The bus finally comes to a screeching stop and I hear Jonny's shout as he nearly rolls off of his seat. The moment the bus comes to a stop, everyone is up on their feet and there's a race to get out of the doors as quickly as possible.

So this is the start of my summer camp experience.

Annie grabs her bags and goes to Jonny's side to offer him a hand up.

"How'd you sleep?" Annie asks. I'm standing behind her now, with my backpack slung over my shoulders. He takes Annie's hand and stretches his arms above his head before he runs a hand through his hair and shakes the sleepiness from himself.

"Like a baby," He replies with a smirk. He glances back at me and I feel my face starting to burn up with the attention. It takes another few minutes for the bus to clear out and we make our way out as a group.

There are small groups of kids still wandering around or chatting but for the most part, everyone is rushing to the two large cabins that are placed on opposite sides of a bonfire pit. It doesn't look like any adults are going to try and control the group.

"I'll see you guys soon, girls sleep in different cabins than boys." Annie gives us a wave before rushing off to the cabin on the right. It seems like everyone's in a silent agreement to rush to the cabins for some reason.

I turn to look at Jonny. He still looks tired with faint dark circles under his eyes and his hair starting to stick out at odd angles because of his nap. He still seems to be waking up, though, so I glance around at the place that's going to be my home for the next two weeks.

Besides the two cabins, there is no sign of civilization. The forest that surrounds us is impossible to see into past a few dozen feet before the world blurs into different shades of green and brown. There's the calming sound of rustling leaves and a stream somewhere nearby.

It smells clean. Fresh. I adore it.

"We can bunk together if you'd like," Jonny says finally. I turn to look at him and find myself staring into his eyes. He must have been watching me and I nod, trying to hide my embarrassment from him. I really need to break the habit of zoning out around him. He seems to catch me at the worst moments.

"Oh, is that… are you okay with that?" I stammer. I don't know why, since he's the one that offered it.

"I'd rather share a room with you than some random asshole," He says with a smile. I relax a little bit and he nods to the cabin on the left. "Come on, before everyone takes the good rooms."

I follow close behind him as we walk through the cabin. Most of the rooms are already taken up by people who are unpacking or just fucking around for the most part. It takes a little while but I manage to find an empty room that's far enough from everyone else that we might actually manage to get some sleep.

"I think this is the best we can do," I say after looking in. There's one bunk bed, a small bathroom, and one chest of drawers but besides that, it's completely empty. Jonny looks around the room and nods his approval before he walks in.

"So you've never been out in the woods before?" He asks. I shake my head as I follow into the room behind him and swing my backpack off. I can feel his eyes studying me and with jerky, nervous movements I start to unpack my backpack into the wardrobe. Anything to distract me from his intense gaze.

"No, not really. I… I'm not really all into the outdoors." I stammer. My body doesn't feel like my own as I unpack the last of my clothes into a single drawer and then gently slide it shut. I rush to the bunk beds and toss my backpack up onto the top bunk.

I watch as Jonny makes his way to the wardrobe, opens a different drawer, and dumps all of his clothes into a drawer, and slides it shut. He drops his backpack onto the floor next to the drawer before he spins around to look at me again.

"What are you into?" He asks. There's something in his voice that makes my breath catch in my throat. His voice is almost a purr and my mind goes blank, leaving me scrambling to say anything at all.

"I… I like reading. And… um… I don't know, I like school for the most part." I cringe at how boring it makes me sound. I don't know how Jonny manages to seem so cool and calm at all times but he's the type that's a loner. He manages to just… exist in the way that he wants to. That's part of the reason that I can't seem to get over this crush on him.

"Well, that's good. You and Annie will get along. She's obsessed with reading and she's pretty damn smart." He offers. When we were on the bus, Annie and I spent the entire two hours talking. She's actually a pretty cool kid, in her own way. She dresses the way she wants, she knows more about nature than anyone else I've ever met, and she's incredibly curious about everything and anything. She's easy company, which is exactly the type of company I prefer.

Jonny, on the other hand, is not easy company. He's a bit confusing, a bit mysterious, and very very intimidating. I feel my curiosity starting to rise.

This is the first real time we've interacted outside of the few classes we had together. I never really got to know anything about him. It was all rumors from other kids.

"What about you? What do you do for fun?" I ask. He lets out a little huff of laughter and smirks at me again. His eyes lock on me again and he looks me up and down with the ghost of something… amused in his expression.

"I get into a lot of trouble. I spray paint stuff, I help Annie collect cool wildness things for her collection, I like getting into fights." He lists. It's the stuff I've heard about him. That he's trouble and he has problems with authority and that he disappears into the woods for days sometimes.

"Trouble? Like, have you been arrested?" I ask. I'm not sure if it's a good idea to ask him about his criminal record but now that I have a chance to get to know him, the years of quiet adoration are overcoming my nervousness.

"No, not yet at least. And not just legal shit. I get in trouble with a lot of people." He shrugs. I don't know how he manages to say it so casually, but that must just be the norm in his mind. God knows that he lives a different life than I do.

"Who else, besides the police?"

"The church. Parents. Girls. Guys."

I freeze. Guys. Does that mean anything? Or is that just his way of teasing me? Does he know about me from the rumors at school?

He glances over at me and gives me another smile. My knees go weak and I realize that I've been staring and look away.

"Oh." I finally breathe.

But before I can try and compose myself, Jonny takes a step towards me. I immediately take a step back and the backs of my knees hit the edge of the bed. I fall backward onto the mattress and I find myself sprawled on the bed, looking up at Jonny's amused expression. My breathing is coming in short, shallow gasps and I know that my face is bright red at this point.

"What about you? You get into any trouble?" He asks in that soft purr of a voice. My entire body shivers at the sound and I stare at him. He's definitely teasing at this point but I don't know how to act around him. "Come on, this is what guys talk about. Don't worry about it."

I've never really had guy friends before, but I'm certain that they don't do this. They don't ask about getting into trouble with boys while one of them is lying on a bed with the other's eyes on them. This isn't what guys do.

"No. Not really, I don't… I don't get into trouble." I whisper. I take the moment to study his face again. He's tall, and his black shirt clings to his body to show off his muscular frame. He's got piercing icy blue eyes and his curly hair is falling around his face now that it's not in a ponytail.

My stomach is twisted up in knots and I feel arousal burning in my stomach.

"Well, goody two shoes, let's hope it stays that way." He says, taking a step backward. I stay laying on the bed for another moment and get to my feet. "Let's head out, people are gonna be waiting for us outside."

What is happening? What was that? My mind is racing with thoughts, my heart still pounding in my chest.

"Do we want to be out there with other people?" I ask. Jonny has never been a social or popular kid and I want to avoid the rest of the campers at any cost. They're exactly the type that I've been dodging my entire high school life.

"I wanna get dinner is what I want." He says, holding the door open for me. I take a shaky breath and slip past him, out of our room.

Chapter 3

"Hey! How are you liking everything so far?" Annie asks. She came bounding out of the girl's cabin without her backpack. Instead, she's holding an old, worn-out-looking journal in her arms that she's pressed up against her chest. She's changed out of her colorful clothes in favor of a pair of dull green overalls and a plain undershirt. She looks more wilderness-ready than anyone else.

"I've only been here for like an hour."

I don't want to mention anything about anything Jonny did yet. I don't know how she would react and more than that, I want him to do that to me again. Just thinking about it makes my breathing catch in my throat and I fumble for another answer that'll cover the blush I can feel creeping onto my face.

"I like it. I've never been out in the woods like this before." That part, at least, is true. It's my first time in the woods and I have to admit there's something very soothing about being surrounded by trees and the sounds of the wild. Annie nods, her curly ponytail wagging with her movements.

"Your parents never took you camping?" She asks. She begins to walk to a shelter that I didn't notice before. It's nothing more than a roof balanced on four metal beams and it looks like everyone is gravitating towards there.

I shake my head. My parents were never really that involved in my life. It's part of the reason they jumped on the opportunity to send me here, to get me off of their back.

"What about you?" I ask. During the bus ride, at least, it seemed like Annie was used to attending these sorts of things and she seemed to know a lot about the place we were going to be staying. Her face lights up at the questions and she begins one of her excited ramblings.

"Oh, my dad's a park ranger. He used to take me out to the woods all the time. It's why I was allowed into the high schooler's summer camp programs when I was in middle school. Plus, I get to help him a little by tracking the flora in the area around the camps." Annie points to her journal and I can see now that there are little bits of paper sticking out. It's obvious to see that it's an old journal that she's been using for years.

"That's how you met Jonny?" I can't help but want to know more about him. Yes, we had classes together and now we're going to be living together for the next two weeks but I still don't really know much about him. He's trouble, he's flirty, he's... oddly patient with me. But besides that, I don't know a single thing about him.

"Yeah. He was the only one that was nice to me." Annie says. I've picked on that so far. He doesn't seem like the type to bully without reason but there's definitely an air of power and danger to him. Usually, I would avoid people like that like the plague. This time, I feel drawn to him.

"Well, that's nice." I nod. I'm close enough to hear the chatter from the shelter and the smell of food is wafting through the air. I didn't even realize I was hungry until this moment and now that my anxiety has faded, I realize that I'm starving.

"Come on. Let's go grab some food."

We make our way into a shelter, where a large table is set up with trays of food. I hesitate for a moment before Annie grabs a paper plate and hands it to me. I begin to pile on food, trying not to think of all the unwashed hands that had just grabbed at the food or used the tongs.

"Don't touch that." Someone grabs my wrist as I reach out to a tray of mac n cheese. I look up to see Jonny at my side, holding my wrist in his grasp. I'm staring again and my entire body goes hot.

Does he know what he's doing? Does he have me figured out? And does he even care about people seeing us like this?

"Why not?" I try to twist my arm out of his grip. He doesn't budge at all and I feel panic and arousal rising in my chest. He holds onto me for another few seconds, almost to make a point, before he lets me go.

"The older kids have a messed up tradition of putting stuff in there. Rocks and dirt and stuff." He says. Now that I'm looking at it, I notice that no one else has touched the tray of mac n cheese. A few people are looking at me expectantly and my hand pulls away like I've been burned. "Once we found a squirrel in there."

"Oh, gross," I say, stepping away from the table. The thought of it makes me shiver and I've lost my appetite.

"Come on. Let's go sit down." Jonny says and I follow behind him. I've noticed that the bullies and populars tend to stay out of his way. There's something about the way that they all scatter when he walks towards them that tells me that he's probably gotten in trouble with them before.

"Hey! Lost you there for a moment." Annie bumps into me, balancing her plate of food on top of her journal. I relax with her presence.

Jonny is interesting and attractive and… mysterious but Annie is open and curious and bubbly. They seem like opposites but somehow they manage to work together. And somehow, I've found myself grouped up with them.

"Yeah, sorry about that. Jonny made sure that I didn't eat any rocks or squirrels, though." I say. With Annie standing right next to us, I feel Jonny lean against me. He's taller than me by half a foot and he's bigger and more muscular. I nearly topple over and bump into Annie before I manage to right myself.

"That's good. It's a real hazard." Annie says and without missing a beat, starts to explain more about the summer camp. It seems like she's excited to be the one in charge for once and not the baby of her little friend group. "Usually the first night, everyone eats at the bonfire. Just so that the camp counselors can keep track of us."

I notice the few logs that are placed around the bonfire. Already, people are sitting around the fire. Now that I've noticed that, I also notice that there's a big fire burning in the center of the ring.

"I haven't really seen any of them. Where are they?" I ask. There wasn't anyone who looked like an adult even on the bus and now that I look around, I can't see anyone in uniform. Honestly, Jonny is probably the oldest looking one out of all of us.

"Oh? The camp counselors are all just college kids. Most of the time they're sleeping or they're goofing off with us." Annie points to a few people wandering around. They honestly don't look much older than us and none of them have made a move to keep track of us or even try to establish order. So far, it's been a free for all.

"And they let us get away with anything we want." Jonny leans down, whispering that into my ear. A feeling of heat rising in my stomach and my back arches. My eyes are darting around to see if anyone has noticed us, but no one is paying any attention to us.

And as quickly as it happened, Jonny stands up again and it's almost like he didn't say anything to me at all. I don't know what he's trying to do, but this crush I've had on him for years is hitting me all over again.

It's leaving me absolutely breathless and fucking nervous as hell.

"Yeah. It's pretty fun." Annie says, shrugging. Apparently, she hasn't noticed anything, either.

"Yeah," I say, holding back a shuddering breath.

Chapter 4

"So… what do we do now?" I ask.

All three of us have finished our food and the sun is just now starting to set. The darkness is thicker here in the woods than it ever was back home because the trees are looming over us, blocking the last minutes of sunlight.

A few camp counselors have piled up wood on the bonfire and it's the only light we have in the middle of the woods. All of the campers are still outside, trying to huddle close to the fire to keep from freezing in the steady night breeze. Thankfully, we sat pretty close to the middle, to begin with, and I'm feeling toasty warm.

"We stay out. Listen to ghost stories. Just try to stay close to the campsite for the next few days and then the counselors usually stop caring." Annie says. She's opened up her journal and is jotting down a few notes with impressively detailed sketches of different leaves and plant stems that she's picked off of the ground. She's lost in her own world of focus and I find myself turning to Jonny for answers instead.

"Don't people go missing?" I ask. It's a silly worry to have but it's a thought that won't leave me alone.

And apparently, I'm not the only one that's thinking about it.

"People are going missing?" A girl gasps a few feet away from me. Jonny and I both turn to look at her but it's impossible to tell who said it in the crowd of faces behind us.

Almost immediately, the dozen or so conversations that had been going on before all come to a screeching stop. All eyes are on me and I feel my palms start to sweat.

"No, no that's not what I-" I begin to fumble over my words but someone else in the crowd shouts something.

"He's right, people do go missing at these summer camps! Like Robbie, a few years back?" It's a boy's voice and there's an edge of something cruel in his words. A murmur rips through the crowd and I can almost physically feel the nervousness hanging in the air. Would I get in trouble for spreading rumors? Or would I be held responsible if there was a camp-wide panic tonight?

"He was an idiot and he was high off of his ass. He didn't go missing, he just went home." Jonny's voice rings through the air. It cuts off everyone's anxious thoughts and everyone is staring at him. He stares right back with an air of confidence that puts me at ease. Of course, Jonny would know what to say in this situation.

"But what about Alex?" Some other kid says. Jonny laughs at the mention of the name.

"He was kicked out because he was trying to organize an orgy."

"What about the missing people recently?" This time, it's a boy sitting not too far away from us. He's one of the shy kids and his face goes bright red when he sees everyone looking at him and he rushes to explain himself. "Not in this summer camp but… these woods have been having a lot of people go missing in them recently."

Annie's the one to jump in with an explanation this time. She snaps her journal shut and stands up, commanding everyone's attention as she delivers a short speech to the few dozen nervous campers.

"Well, compared to other state parks in this part of the country, we aren't actually doing too bad. Plus, it's summer. People go out hiking in this area and the most popular ones go up into the mountains where there's no service and it takes a long while to come back down. Usually, people miscalculate and tell people they'll be back sooner than realistic." It almost sounds rehearsed with how certain she is of herself. Of course, Annie's father is a park ranger and she would know that sort of thing. She turns to the boy who had first brought it up and gives him a reassuring smile. "I wouldn't worry about it too much."

The boy smiles back, looking a little less nervous than he had just a minute ago.

Annie's only fourteen years old but in moments like these, it's easier to forget that she's two years younger than me. She's so much more confident than I am. There's no way in hell I would ever voluntarily stand in front of a group of people and talk to them in the way that she does.

"Isn't this park an Indian graveyard?" Someone else asks. The teasing is over for the most part and the question doesn't seem like anyone is trying to cause any trouble. With Annie standing, giving out actual answers, makes all of them feel a little safer.

"It's Indigenous land, yes, but if we're being realistic most of America is a graveyard." She explains gently. The murmuring starts up again and I can tell that her answers helped to calm everyone down. She stays standing for another few moments, waiting for more questions. When there are none, she sits back down and opens up her journal again, picking up a little sketch of a maple leaf that she plucked off the ground a while ago.

"That was impressive," I whisper to both of them. Although Annie doesn't look up from her drawing, I can tell that she's smiling.

"There's a difference between ghost stories and spreading rumors. Plus, it's disrespectful to the Indigenous people." She says simply. I nod and watch her finish up her drawings and notes for the next few minutes.

The conversation does pick up again but it's tamer now. There are some standard ghost stories and local cryptid stories that people bring up but it's all for fun rather than to scare anyone. The sun is long gone and the fire is starting to die down by the time the conversation starts to turn serious again.

"Well… Have you heard of what's making people go missing?" Someone prompts. It's not like the other scary stories that people have been telling up until this point. I glance at Annie and Jonny but they seem to brush it off for the moment. I trust that they'll jump in if it gets too bad.

"There's a thing that the Indigenous talk about. The spirit of the dead." The quiet boy says. It's too dark to see him well anymore but I can tell that he's cold. His arms are wrapped around himself and he's shaking like a leaf. I can hear it in his voice.

When no one says anything in response, he continues to talk. His voice is hushed and tired but it still somehow manages to carry in the still night air. No one has to strain to hear him.

"It lures people into the woods to the places where Indigenous people were killed. Like a soul for a soul type of thing." He says. The night air seems to cool another few degrees at the sound of his voice and it's impossible to ignore him now. Even though he's not shouting, it seems like he's getting louder. Or closer. "It lives in the treetops and sounds like the howling of the wolves that used to live in this area."

"What does it look like?"

"No one has survived to describe it."

The silence seems to come crashing back over all of us. It takes a long while before I can even suck in a breath of air and when I finally do, it burns in my lungs like smoke. There seemed to be an edge of a threat in the boy's words but before any of us can ask, he gets up and heads back to the sleeper cabins.

"Alright, well that was the third or fourth-best ghost story campfire I've been to," Jonny says with my heart still pounding in my chest. I don't want anyone to know how much that actually scared me.

He stands up, stretching his arms above his head. I catch a glimpse of pale skin as his shirt rides up his stomach. There's the contour of his abs and the happy trail that creeps up his stomach. His arms are flexed and I can see the muscles tensed and trembling.

And then I realize that he's caught me staring again and I look away.

Shit.

"Come on." He offers me a hand up that I reluctantly take. I don't know why he's putting up with me, especially with the way I'm acting but he doesn't seem to care much. Instead, he turns to Annie and waves. "Goodnight Annie, I promise we can try and find something for you tomorrow."

"Of course. Goodnight Jonny, goodnight Connor." She says, giving us both a wave goodnight. We walk away from the circle around the bonfire. The darkness settles around us and seems to usher us away from everyone else in the world.

"You weren't actually scared by that, were you?" He asks once we're out of earshot.

"N-No," I say, but the stutter ruins whatever weak attempt at bravery there was in my voice.

"Good."

Chapter 5

It's been an entire hour since I went to bed and I still can't even begin to doze off. All of the silly talks about ghosts and monsters are a little harder to brush off as a joke now that I'm lying here, alone, in the dark.

But I'm not really alone. I'm on the top bunk and just a few feet away from me, Jonny is sound asleep. It only makes my face burn up with embarrassment at the thought. He's able to play everything off and handle situations that I can't even stand to be in. I've been trying to stay still for the last hour to make sure I don't wake him up.

I decide to just accept that tonight is going to be a bad night. Hopefully tomorrow, I'll be able to sleep a little better. I'm staring up at the darkness above my head where there's supposed to be a roof when I hear his voice.

"Are you asleep?" It's definitely Jonny's voice coming from below me and my heart nearly stops in my chest. I don't know how he knows since I've been as still as a statue and I was sure that he fell asleep ages ago.

The seconds slip by before I make up my mind. I can't really lose anything by having a conversation with Jonny.

"Nope. You alright?"

"Oh, I'm fine. I'm just having a hard time going to sleep." He doesn't sound particularly bothered by it by any means. I nod up to the darkness above my face, trying to keep the images out of my mind. The mental pictures of his stomach, his face, his toned body keeps on playing in my head now that I know he's awake.

"Yeah, me too," I say, hoping that my voice isn't shaking as much as I think it is.

"Do you wanna come sleep in my bed?" Jonny asks immediately. I freeze on my bed, wondering if I heard that right. Is he joking? Jonny doesn't seem like the type to joke or tease me about that kind of thing. Or does he know about my crush on him? Is this some sort of test?

"Really?" I ask. I'm starting to sweat now, feeling on edge. My heart is racing in my chest and I can't stop my anxious thoughts from running through my head at full speed. Every single fear I've had of being outed as gay is rushing back to me but…

It's Jonny. And for Jonny, the guy I've had a crush on since the beginning of high school. The guy I'm just now getting to know for the first time. The guy who's surprisingly sweet for the way that he looks and acts.

"Sure. I don't mind you sleeping with me, especially after those stories." Jonny's voice is starting to get raspy and I shiver. It's probably because he's tired but my body reacts without thinking.

"They didn't scare me," I say quickly. I don't want him thinking I'm some child that needs to be protected but he laughs at me anyways. With our two year age difference and our differing personalities, I imagine that he doesn't see me as anything more than a kid.

"It's okay if it did. I used to get nightmares, too." He says. There's something in his voice that's open. Vulnerable. I stay lying on my back on my bed for a moment before I get up and carefully climb down the ladder. The floor is cold against my feet and I walk to his bed.

"Hey." I can barely see him in the dim light but I can hear him move under his sheets. He lifts the blanket for me to crawl in with him. I hesitate only for a moment before I slip into bed with him, leaving enough space between the both of us so that we aren't touching. I'm as tense as can be as I lie with him, wondering how on earth I'm going to fall asleep when my heart is racing in my chest just by being near him,

"If you want to cuddle, I don't mind. I like it, actually." Jonny says. I jump when I hear how close he is to me. He must have inched closer and, if I focus, I can feel his breath against my neck. There's a faint warm radiating from behind me that I know is his body.

"I don't want to make you do anything," I say. I don't know how to tell him yes. I want to beg for him to touch me.

"You're not making me do anything. I'm the one that brought it up." He whispers back. I hear the sheets move again and then feel his arms wrap around me, pulling me close against his body. I turn to face him. It's still too dark to see him well in the darkness, even with how close I am to him.

I know that he's muscular, but I've never touched him. There's something a little surprising about how soft his body is when he's relaxed, the warmth that radiates off of him, the smell of the woods, and his cologne mixing together. I'm frozen for a moment before I take a deep breath and start to melt into his touch.

I feel… safe.

His hands rub small patterns on my back and I feel myself start to relax. His body is pressed up against mine and I can feel the rise and fall of his chest. My head is resting on his arm, which is a surprisingly good pillow. I'm just starting to drift off when I feel heat start to pool in my stomach and I realize what's happening.

"Oh, I'm sorry." I gasp, scooting away from him. I didn't even realize I was getting hard until that moment and I feel my face burning up with embarrassment. He definitely felt it with the way that our legs were tangled up together and I was pressed against his thigh.

"It's fine. It's normal and it's not the first time." He says, his arms still wrapped around me. He hasn't stopped making those little patterns up and down my back and now that I'm starting to wake up again and I can't stop my racing thoughts.

It's not the first time. He's… like me?

"You've… done this with guys?" I ask. He pulls me close against his body again and this time it feels less innocent. His thigh is in between my legs again and the way that he pulls me in makes me gasp.

"Yeah. None as cute as you, though." He whispers to me. His voice has definitely dropped an octave and gained a roughness to it that makes me shiver. He's hugging me close to him and my body is responding to his touch. I feel warm, throbbing all over with my pulse pounding in my veins.

And then he rolls his hips. I feel something hard press against my thigh and I let out a small sound of surprise in the back of my throat.

"Oh." I gasp. He's hard, too.

The thought of Jonny. In bed with me. Hard. Grinding up against my thigh. Holding me against him. It's overwhelming and I wonder for a moment if this is actually all just a dream I'm having. But no, the feeling of his bulge pressing against my thigh, hot and rock hard, is too real to be a dream.

"Is this alright? We don't need to do anything if you don't want to." He asks. His voice is getting rougher and it makes my heart skip a few beats. I don't know exactly what he wants to do but I would let him do just about anything to me right now. Anything to make him feel good.

"No, please. I… I want this." I say. I surprise myself with the way that I sound. My voice is high and whiny and almost sounds needy with the way that I say "please". Jonny's arms wrap around me tighter and he presses his lips against my forehead.

"Alright, just relax. I'll take care of you." He says.

And in an instant, he flexes his arms and suddenly I'm under him. He's straddling me, his thighs trapping me under him and his arms pressed against the mattress as he holds himself up. The bed is dipping under his weight and I feel dizzy with how fast he moves.

"Oh!" I yelp. He chuckles and I feel my blood start to burn when I realize that he's just as hard as I am. I can feel his erection rubbing against my stomach and he shuffles around, positioning himself in between my thighs before he grinds back down on me.

I gasp, arching my back off of the mattress. It's the first time I've done anything like this and the adrenaline does nothing but heightens the pleasure. It's coursing through my body now, making me feel warm and fuzzy all over as my mind goes completely blank and all I can do is gasp for breath

"Relax. It'll feel better if you relax. And don't worry, I want to take my time with you." Jonny almost growls. His hands press against my thighs and then trail up, making me tremble before his fingers hook over the hem of my pants. Even in the dark, he doesn't have a problem taking off my pants and then yanking my boxers down to my knees.

I feel the mattress drip and I feel him move and all of a sudden, he's touching me again. It's a bit confusing to try and figure out what is going on when the lights are off but the darkness puts me on edge and every brush of skin we have is like electricity burning through my body.

First, his lips on mine. It's my first kiss ever, and when he presses his tongue into my mouth I feel something hard against my lip. His mouth moves expertly against my inexperienced lips and he carefully guides me through the kiss.

Eventually, I give up on trying to match him and go limp. He doesn't seem to mind, since his tongue is still exploring my mouth, then my neck, and finally biting down on my collarbone.

"It's my tongue piercing." He says when he finally pulls back. I'm almost too far gone to hear him but when the words sink in I let out a feeble little whine. Of course, he had piercings but I didn't know about that particular one.

"Alright, let me just…" Jonny moved again, pushing my thighs apart. My body is trembling with anticipation before I feel something press down on my crotch and my entire body feels alive with the sensation of our bodies moving together.

"Ah!" My hands go to his arms to brace myself as he continues rolling his hips. I've never felt anything this intense. I thought stuff like this would just be like jerking off but it's almost completely different. Jonny's able to coax moans out of me and make my entire body tremble easily.

I'm starting to feel lightheaded when he wraps a hand around both of us and gives both of us a quick stroke. My body is thrown into a spasm and I weakly try to thrust up into his hand and against his length.

"Oh, that's really cute. Do it again." Jonny mutters, giving us both another stroke. This time, I can't bite back my moans and I let out a loud groan.

"Ah!" I'm breathless, gasping for air as he speeds up. I feel myself being pushed to the edge and grit my teeth. I don't want it to end and I tense my entire body to try and slow down my body's natural urges.

"Come on, you've been a good boy. You deserve a reward." Jonny says in the darkness. His free hand reaches up my shirt and his hand presses against my chest as he continues to stroke both of us off. My skin is burning hot and soaked with sweat as he rolls his hips at the perfect rhythm to match his strokes.

"Jonny. Jonny, please." I moan without thinking. I don't know what I'm begging for anymore but the pressure is building in the pit of my stomach and it's nearly unbearable. I keep on squirming, thing to find something missing to finally find my release.

"Yeah? Come on, be good for me." I can almost hear Jonny's voice. His touch becomes rougher against my chest and his other hand is jerking us off quickly. His hard erection is pressed against mine and I can tell that he's chasing his orgasm now.

I have to hear him gasp and then let out a shuddering moan before I'm following his lead. My entire body clenches down and I press my body back into the mattress, shuddering as my orgasm washes over me. I can feel him finish on my stomach and chest and I know that our cm is both splattered onto my skin.

"Oh, fuck!" I shout, my nails digging into Jonny's back. It takes a few moments before I realize I must be hurting him and I let my hands fall to the side. We stay still for a few moments before Jonny shifts, letting go of us and reaching over. I feel him wiping me off with what feels like a tee-shirt before he lies back down next to me.

"Alright, alright. I think that's enough for one night." He whispers. My entire body feels warm and light at the promise of this happening again and his arms wrap around me. "Feeling alright?"

I can't even find the energy to respond. Instead, I make a little sound at the back of my throat and snuggle up against his chest. His hands cradle me and then work up to play with my hair.

"I'll take that as a yes." His voice is gentle and he presses a kiss to my forehead. "Goodnight, Connor."

I don't have any nightmares that night.

Chapter 6

I wake up in Jonny's arms.

"Wake up. We gotta get ready." He's gently shaking my shoulders but it still takes me a moment to realize what's happening.

I jump when I realize that I'm cuddling with him. And that I must have slept in his bed last night. And then the memories rush in and I realize that we did much more than that.

"Are you alright?" He asks. The worry is obvious in his voice and my anxiety starts to melt away. As scary as Jonny can be sometimes, he's a sweetheart.

"Oh, yeah. It was… That was the first time I've done that with anyone." I whisper. I try to hide my face from him, knowing that the blush on my cheeks is probably some shade of red by now.

He gives me a soft pat to the head before he untangles himself from me and rolls out of bed. Now that he isn't holding me, the tiredness slips away and I sit up, admiring him. He's still swearing his boxers but besides that, he's naked. His body is toned and he's pulling his curly hair into a small ponytail, which shows off the muscles in his arms.

"You were perfect. Maybe we can do it again tonight if you want?" He suggests.

"Yes, please."

We shower, brush our teeth and get dressed together before walking out of our room together. There's still dew on the grass from last night and a thick fog has rolled over the woods and it's hard to tell if the sun is up yet and I glance around.

It's oddly quiet. And there are more people out than there are usually. A group of boys sits near the bonfire we all sat at yesterday and I stare at them. They're not talking. They don't seem to be eating. They're all just standing there, the silhouettes of their bodies hard to tell apart from each other. The fog makes them look like a jumbled pile of arms, legs, and scowling faces.

"So… What do we do today?" I ask, not taking my eyes off of the group of boys. I don't know if it's the fog or the stories from last night or the fact that I'm certain they're all popular boys that makes me feel on edge but it doesn't matter.

Something is wrong.

"Well… Usually, I find Annie and we grab breakfast…" Jonny starts to say before he trails off. They're moving towards us and now that they're closer, I can see that it's a group of six or seven popular boys. They're the kids with anger issues and sports scholarships that are sent here by their parents and I immediately feel defensive. Jonny steps forward. "What's up?"

They keep on walking towards me and Jonny puts out his hand and pushes me behind him. My heart starts to race and my eyes are scanning my surroundings, looking for someplace to run. But there's nothing but foggy forests surrounding us.

"You two seem really close. Especially last night." One of them stepped up. It's a familiar face, but I can't place a name to him but I know enough about him. I feel my muscles tense, ready to spring into action at any moment. "We heard you. All of it."

My blood goes cold in my veins. I know exactly what he's talking about and I know now that we're in serious danger. Jonny's still standing in front of me, shielding me, but I can see that he's scared too. He's not shaking but his breathing is rapid and his entire body is tense.

"Jonny and I weren't doing-" I begin to say before Jonny cuts me off.

"And what about it?" He spits out. There's real anger in his voice but I can tell that he's not trying to start a fight. He's trying whatever he can to make them back off.

"It's fucking disgusting." The boy says. Jonny takes a step back and I can tell that he's getting ready to run. My feet move back and I position them to run into the woods.

But I'm not leaving without Jonny. There's no way that he'll be able to hold off all seven of them. We both have to run.

"Unlike you? I bet that you've never made a girl cum. Try out guys for once, maybe that's your expertise." Jonny shouts. In one fluid motion, he turns, grabs my wrist, and bolts into the woods with me.

My lungs start to burn as we run through the forest, dodging trees that appear out of nowhere from the fog. I have to catch myself from stumbling a few times and I can barely manage to keep myself on my feet with the damp grass under my feet.

I can hear the shouting behind us and it's only getting closer. There's a film of cold sweat pouring down my face and my grip digs into Jonny's wrist as I start to lag behind.

My legs are about to give out when someone grabs me and I feel my arm get yanked out of Jonny's grip. In just a second, I'm lifted off the ground and I'm thrashing, trying to get away from the boy that's holding me up.

"Jonny!" I shout as the arms tighten around me, crushing my chest and making it impossible to breathe. Jonny turns around and with a running start, slams into the boy. I crash to the ground and only catch another glimpse of Jonny kicking the boy while he's down.

The smell of iron and the sounds of shouting are in the air as I stare at him. I don't want to leave him but through the fog, I can see the six other boys gaining on us.

"Connor run!" Jonny shouts. I feel my body instinctively want to follow his directions but I hesitate. There's no way that Jonny can fight all of them and with one of them on the ground, bleeding and unconscious, I know that they'll kill him if they have the chance to.

"But-" I start to say.

"RUN!"

The words echo through the woods, booming in my ears before I turn and sprint in a random direction. I fight back the tears welling up in my eyes and the burning in my throat from my gasping.

I left him. I left him there to die. The guilt is almost overwhelming as I flee through the woods, expecting to hear the shouting die down.

Instead, I can hear it getting closer. I look over my shoulder to see that five boys are still running after me, hot on my trail.

Chapter 7

I'm dry heaving, bracing myself against the cool, wet stone cliff I'm standing next to. I know I should keep on running but my body is ready to give out. My muscles are shaky and burning with the strain I just put myself from. My throat is burning and my vision is blurry with tears as I heave but my stomach is empty. There's nothing to vomit.

It takes what feels like hours for me to recover but I eventually manage to stand up. I have to lean against the rock cliff I'm hiding against and take a moment to look around.

The forest looks different here. It's lush and green here, mostly because of the stream that's cascading over the edge of this cliff, making a small waterfall and pooling at the base.

My throat is dry and burning and the sight of the clear water is enough to make me move again. I have to be careful moving on the slippery rock but I eventually make it to the edge of the pool and collapse. The water is cold and soothes my throat as I gulp it down, not caring if it's safe to drink or not.

After I drink enough to quench my throat, all the strength leaves my body. The adrenaline that's been pushing me this entire time is gone now and I lay on the ground, feeling the cool stone against my cheek as I breathe slowly. I'm about to fall asleep to the sound of the waterfall ringing in my ears when I hear something rise above it.

I try and ignore it as my body tries to slip into unconsciousness. I want so badly to fall asleep but the sound grows louder and louder.

"Connor! Connor!" It's someone's panicked voice and when I hear it I feel a bit of strength returning. They're getting closer now and I get to my feet unsteadily.

"Connor, where are you?" I hear Jonny's voice and my mind clears enough to form thoughts again.

"Here! I'm here!" I shout back. It burns my throat to speak and it's nearly unbearable to shout like that but just a few seconds after I shout, I see a flicker of movement, and then Annie leaps into view and throws her arms around me. She hugs me tight for a moment before letting me go, stepping back and holding me at arm's length, and looking me over.

"Are you alright?" She asks. The relief that I feel is making my knees weak and I have to lean against the rock cliff again to steady myself.

"Yeah. I'm fine." I breathe. I don't know how I managed to unrun all of them but eventually, I lost all of them. It's a miracle, too. Who knows what could have happened if they caught me. They're somewhere in the woods, blindly wandering around, trying to find me.

Jonny slips into view and I stumble into his arms.

"Connor." His voice is sad and angry and tired but I understand all of the unspoken words between the two of us. I know what he means to say, but can't right now. Still, I cling onto him for a few moments longer before I let him go.

"Where are we?" Jonny asks, looking around. Now that I'm not alone and I had something to drink, things aren't looking so bleak. Annie glances around and I can see her mind racing.

"Well, we're quite a distance away from camp but-" She begins to say before a rumbling cuts her off. We all pause, looking around. It isn't the waterfall, but it was a similar sound only much, much louder.

"What is that." I point over Annie's shoulder into the thickest parts of the forest. With the fog, it's hard to see that far but I can see something moving. Maybe it's just the wind blowing branches around but I can swear that I can see whole trees shifting around.

"Probably a deer. The biggest thing that lives here is the black bear and-" Annie starts to talk again and stops. We're all watching that spot that I pointed out and I see it again.

Whole trees moving. Being uprooted, bending like they have joints in them. The sound of splintering, creaking wood rises above the sound of the waterfall. Jonny reaches out, taking my hand again like he did when he saw that gang for the first time.

"That's not a bear," I whisper. It's definitely nothing natural. My hair is standing on end and again, the numbing adrenaline is flooding my system. My body is trembling with exhaustion but I'm somehow able to find another wave of energy.

"What do we do?" Jonny asks. The fear is evident in his voice and it makes me shiver. Even when we were up against those seven boys, there wasn't a hint of fear in his voice.

"Move slowly. Be careful." Annie's voice is shaking and we all take her advice. It's slow work, walking backward with our eyes glued on the movement but after a minute we're back on stable dirt and off of the smooth wet rock.

And then the movements become more coordinated. The trees lift off of the ground, with dirt still caught in the tangle of roots. They're weaving together at the branches to create something that looks like a body that's held up by dozens of tree trunks.

And then we see the glowing eyes turn and stare at us.

"Run!" Jonny shouts and all of us turn, sprinting into the woods again. Annie leads the way, cutting a way through the forest that's much easier to navigate than my random, desperate flight through the woods. Jonny and I trail behind her.

"What is that?"

"I don't know!" Jonny shouts back. His breathing is coming in deep, heavy pants as we run through the woods. I glance over my shoulder and I don't see anything moving but I don't trust my eyes enough to stop running. We run for a few minutes before we all begin to slow down and finally come to a stop.

Jonny and I are doubled over, gasping for air while Annie is staring into the woods with a critical eye. She gives us a few minutes to recover and I raise my head to study her face.

The fear is gone. She looks determined.

"What do we do?" I ask. Annie turns to me, assessing the situation before she pulls out a walkie-talkie from one of her overall pockets.

"I need to talk to my dad."

Chapter 8

"Dad," Annie says in a relieved voice, walking towards an older man in a ranger's uniform. He's dark-skinned with curly, long hair that's tied back into a poofy ponytail and a worried look on his face as he steps forward and scoops up his daughter into his arms.

"Annie, girly, what's going on?" He asks, holding her and then looking at Jonny and me. We're dirty, sweaty, and look exhausted but he ignores it, probably for our sake. "Who is this?"

"This is Connor. We need to talk." Annie nods. I nod to her father and he seems to recognize Jonny right off the bat. Her dad places her on the ground and they walk away.

Jonny and I are left standing alone at the ranger's station. It's been a long hour or so since Annie called up a ranger on her walkie talkie. It took a search party for them to find us and then we were driven here to the only building in this section of the park. It's built to look like a log cabin but thankfully the interior is modernized to have water fountains and AC.

"Are you okay?" Jonny asks. I turn to look at him and I see the exhaustion and fear and anger still burning in his eyes.

This day seems to have stretched on forever. I can't believe that it was just this morning that I had woken up in his arms. Then... everything else happened.

"I don't know," I whisper. The tiredness is seeping into my bones and I slump to the ground, leaning against the floor. Jonny silently sits down next to me and takes my hand. "You saw it too right?"

We were running for ages after seeing that creature move. It hadn't followed us, but none of us felt safe in those woods. Those glowing eyes had definitely seen us, definitely looked at us. It was a creature that was nothing natural.

"Yeah. Yeah, I saw it." Jonny breathes. I hold onto his hand for dear life and I think on it for a moment.

"What do you think it is?" Jonny asks. I pause for a moment but I can't even imagine what it was. I can barely remember it and the memory is getting fuzzy in my mind, despite it being the scariest moment of my life.

"I have no clue. It was weird." I say after another pause. It feels like it was in a dream and the memories are getting harder and harder to grasp the longer I try and focus on it. "Can you remember it well anymore?"

"No. It's weird. I can't remember how it looks anymore." Jonny agrees. I glance up at him and we hold each other's gaze.

I don't know how but something is making us forget about that creature we saw in the woods.

"Okay, so… The seven boys have all gone missing." Annie breaks us out of our daze. Even with her dirty face and her overalls covering a brightly striped shirt, she seems like an adult. "The camp has been informed that we've been found and there are search parties out for them but they can't find them. They should have found them by now with how close they were to the camp in the first place."

She glances between the two of us with a worried look in her eyes. She's managing to hide it better than either of us are and she sits down on the floor in front of us. Her shoulders are hunched and there's a weird look in her face.

"What does your dad think that thing is?" I ask. I don't know what I'm expecting but maybe an adult will have an answer to whatever we saw in the woods. Annie pauses for a moment, fidgeting with the satchel that she's been carrying around.

"He… thinks we were seeing things from the stress. Honestly, that would make sense." She says. I can tell that she doesn't believe it either and I glance at Jonny.

"But we all saw it. The same thing." He says. It's getting more and more difficult to understand exactly what happened in the woods, especially since it was in such a moment of chaos and it was so foggy but with the three of us, I know that we all saw that thing in the woods.

"That's true. But nothing else makes sense." Annie's voice sounds tired and she looks up at both of us. She looks just as lost as us and I remember for the first time in a while that she's younger than us. She doesn't know what's going on.

It seems like no one knows what's going on anymore. We all sit in silence trying to piece it together in our own heads. A memory is trying to push through the haze of my mind before I grab Jonny's hand and gasp.

"But… there was that one kid at the camp. Didn't he say something about this?" I ask. My face flushes with Jonny and Annie's eyes on me but I know it's important.

"The ghost story kid?" Annie asks a bit doubtfully. I know it sounds ridiculous but I have a feeling that he knows something. After all, he was the one to mention something about it the night before all of this happened.

"Yeah. That kid." I say. Annie and Jonny glance at each other and I can see the gears turning in their heads.

"Well… I have no clue. The forest service doesn't know what's going on and… I just don't know." Annie says with a shrug. She's so used to knowing what's going on, knowing what these woods hold, and understanding the world through science and logic. It must be difficult for her to grasp whatever we just survived.

"Well, if those assholes are missing the camp should be a pretty safe bet." Jonny gets to his hand, offering a hand to Annie and helping her up before leaning over me and offering me a hand up. "Do we wanna head back? Talk to that kid?"

I didn't think they would take my idea seriously. I don't even know if it'll get us anywhere but I'd rather be doing something than sit here feeling miserable.

I take Jonny's hand and get to my feet.

"Let's do it."

Chapter 9

It doesn't take long for Annie to track down a park ranger who's willing to drive us back to the camp. She's got a lot of connections here, apparently, and before we know it, we're all crammed into a Jeep and driving back into the woods.

I can feel my heart starting to race in my chest as we get closer to the camp. I'm not sure what the scene will be like when we get back but I'm not looking forward to being at the place where I had to run for my life earlier today.

Just as I'm about to spiral into another panic, Jonny takes my hand. He's watching me and I know that he can see all the fear in my eyes. He leans in and presses a quick kiss to my cheek.

"Alright, here's your stop kiddos!" The car comes to a screeching stop and I nearly slam my head into the seat in front of me.

Not the most romantic moment but it still manages to calm me down.

Annie's the first to open the door and we all scramble out. Even though it's the middle of the afternoon, the fog hadn't lifted at all. Someone has lit the bonfire in an attempt to see better and we all stumble towards it.

"Where have you been Jonny? Someone said the populars tried to kill you!" An older boy steps out of the fog. He's staring back and forth between all three of us with a confused look in his eyes.

"Yeah, that's basically what happened," Jonny says with a shrug before he focuses on the task at hand again. "Do you know where that one kid is? The kid from last night's storytime, the one who was a little weird."

The boy shakes his head and still seems to be processing the fact that we're all alive, in front of him.

"No, not really. I haven't seen him around." He says weakly. Jonny scoffs and starts storming off to the boy's sleeper cabin. Annie and I trail behind him, holding hands. When it comes to dealing with people, it's best to let Jonny do what he needs to do.

He swings open the door and storms into the cabin, shouting at the top of his lungs. Heads poke out of doorways and boys have to scramble out of Jonny's way as he paces back and forth in the hallway.

"Hey! Where's that kid from last night! The one with the weird story!" He shouts. Annie and I stay close to him and watch as he continues to shout, becoming harder and harder to ignore. Even though around a dozen pairs of eyes are watching him shout, no one offers an answer until Jonny starts to kick doors, trying to get them open.

"I think that's his room." Someone says, pointing to a door at the end of the hallway. Jonny glances over and the loose crowd of people flinches away.

"Thanks." He says, turning to Annie and me before walking over to the door. We follow behind him and I feel the hair on the back of my neck start to stand as we get closer to the door.

Jonny goes to knock but the door swings open on contact. He glances towards us and I can't help the shiver that goes down my spine.

Something doesn't feel right about all of this. But Jonny still pushes open the door and slips in.

I follow and find that the room is no different than the room Jonny and I share. There's that same boy, sitting on the bottom bunk bed, watching all three of us enter the room. He has long black hair, tanned skin, and a round face that tells me that he's only about Annie's age at most.

He doesn't seem surprised at all to see three strangers barge into his room after shouting for ages in the hallway.

"Hey. What's your name?" Jonny's voice has the edge of something angry in it. I move to his side and take his hand. We want this kid to be on our side but I can barely hold back my own surging emotions. It's hard not to be angry with all of the chaos and confusion right now.

"Jaci. It's nice to meet you." The boy says, nodding at us evenly. His voice is soothing and I can feel Jonny relax at my side.

"How did you know?" I ask. There's no point in trying to explain the situation but Jaci nods in understanding anyways. It's almost like he can read our minds with the way that nothing seems to surprise him.

"My family lived here, since the very beginning. It's been difficult to watch what happened here." He turns to look at Annie and gives her a grateful smile. "Thank you for standing up for me and my family."

"You're Indigenous?" Annie asks. I remember that night when Annie corrected a few people on their rumors and see the surprise on her face. The boy nods, seeing a little happy to be understood.

"Yes. I came here this year because my sister felt something happening in these woods. People were going missing and the spirits were unhappy with the treatment of the land here." He says all of this like it's a simple fact of life. There's nothing in his voice that tells me that he's lying but it's a lot to try and understand at once.

But... all of this is so crazy. The fading image of the trees being uprooted and the glowing eyes and the spindly limbs being woven out of tree branches flashes across my mind again, making me shiver.

"It was a spirit?" I ask again. Jaci turns to look at me, studying my face, and nods.

"You saw it?"

"Yeah. It's... hard to explain what it looks like." I say. Already, the image is slipping away again but the feeling of blood-chilling fear is still lingering in my system. Jaci nods and there's a worried look on his face as he watches me shiver. I barely feel Annie and Jonny's arms wrap around me, trying to get me to calm down.

"It chose to let you live but it does not want to be discovered. It saw your hearts and saw that you did not mean any harm. It wants to protect this land from colonizers." Jaci explains as I'm slowly pulled out of my panic. I'm still panting and my knees feel ready to give out under me but Jaci continues talking. "The populars that chased you down are likely dead by now."

I don't know how to feel about that. They were awful and they wanted me dead for just being gay but... the thought that seven people are dead in the woods now makes me feel dazed.

"Is there a way to stop it? Or get rid of it?" Annie asks. Jaci thinks on this for a moment, his dark brown eyes seemingly deeper than the ocean as he looks at all three of us. He seems to be trying to make up his mind before he speaks again.

"Is it really in our best interests to get rid of it?"

I pause. If this spirit is real, it's been killing people in the woods. But it didn't kill us. It seems to only be hunting those who mean it and others harm. To Jaci and his family... maybe it isn't a bad thing.

"It's a spirit, right?" Annie asks again.

"Yes."

"Maybe... an exorcism?" She offers, looking between all of us in the room. Jonny and I glance at each other and shrug. I have no clue what could stop a creature like this but it doesn't sound like a bad idea. "Will you help us?"

At Annie's question, Jaci sits up a bit straighter. He's staring past us and he seems to be trying to focus on something... something deep in the woods. It takes him a long moment before he snaps out of his daze and stands us. He's no taller than Annie and only really looks like a child, but right now he's the only other person we can trust.

"I can get my sister and we can see what we can do."

Chapter 10

The woods seem to be darker now and the fog is thick enough to suffocate me. Even with the group of people surrounding me, I can't help but feel alone. There's Jaci and his sister, working together to coax a fire from a pile of sticks and leaves that they've piled up. Annie is talking to her father who is looking around at the scene with a concerned look on his face. A man wearing a long black robe is clutching onto a Bible, muttering words into his clasped hands as he goes through the rosary.

I can't help but stare. The woods gave way to this small clearing and there are the ruins of an ancient house here. It's obvious to see that no one had touched it since the day that it was destroyed. The wood is gnawed away by termites and all that is left is the brick walls that are halfway collapsed in places.

"Do you think this is going to work?" Jonny asks, leaning in. He's been holding my hand since we got here and silently staying by my side.

It's nearly night now. It took ages to get all of this together. Annie had to walkie-talkie her father out to the middle of the woods and convince him to grab a priest. It took another thirty minutes of trekking to get to this place, hidden away in the middle of the woods.

It feels wrong to even be standing here. The air seems heavy and looming above me and the darkness seems to swallow everything up. Maybe it's because the night is starting to fall but I have a feeling that it has to do with Jaci's story.

That this is the ruins of the first house attacked by the Indigenous people here. That it was their way of trying to protect their own homes. That the Natives were slaughtered her and that their spirits wait here, seeking revenge. That the spirit that we saw was their spirits still trying to keep their homes safe.

I shiver again and lean against Jonny. I can't believe that we only met yesterday. Eternities seemed to have passed since then and I know that I wouldn't have survived through today. But he's here now and I'm so, so thankful that he is.

"No clue," I whisper. Jonny sighs and wraps his arms around me, pulling me close to his chest. I can feel his heart pounding in his chest but he doesn't say anything at all except to calm me down.

In the silence, I can hear everyone else talking and moving around.

"Annie, I really don't think-" Annie's father is talking and he sounds worried. I open my eyes to look at him and smile at the sight of Annie and her father talking. She barely comes up to my chin and her father looms over me and yet they're talking to each other like they're both adults.

Annie reaches over to grab her dad's hands and looks up at him.

"I promise. I promise this will work." She says gently. There seems to be a moment of pause before he shakes his head and seems to give in. It doesn't seem like he really believes that this will work at all.

I feel myself waver for a moment. Even with everything I've heard and the things I've seen, I don't know if this will work. It really seems like Annie's dad is only here to entertain this idea to get back to work.

Jaci and Naja get to their feet now that that fire the going steady and head over to Annie before all three of them make their way to us.

Seeing the three of them makes something in my chest drop. Jaci seemed so wise when we were talking but now that he's standing next to his sister and Annie, he looks like just another little boy. And his sister, who had predicted all of this and led us all to this little ruined house, seemed like just another little girl standing next to Annie.

Annie's father steps aside and the priest makes his way towards us with a determined look on his face.

"I think we're ready to begin." He says. His voice is booming and low with something menacing in his voice. We all nod and move to form a semicircle away from the ruins as the priest walks to be in front of the ruins.

It's quiet enough that I can hear his long black robe skim across the dry leaves on the ground and make a gentle rustling. He takes a few deep breaths before raising his arms above his head with the Bible in one hand and his rosary in the other.

"Spirit! I command you to leave this holy place!" He shouts. His voice echoes into the woods for a moment and we all flinch at the sound. In the silence, it seems too dramatic to be real at all. He looks around, though, and then shouts again. "Spirit, show yourself!"

There's another moment of silence. I can feel my pulse starting to race. What if this was all a mistake? What if this wasn't real at all? Maybe we're just wasting everyone's time.

Then there's a rustle from the top of the trees. Then the branches creak and groan and then twist down to touch the ground. Trees begin to uproot themselves and the splintering of wood sounds more like screaming than anything else.

Annie's father is running to her in a flash, scooping her up in his arms as she screams. The priest is standing his ground with his arms waving in the air. He must be shouting but it's completely drowned out by the chaos in the world around us.

"Connor!" Jonny shouts. The ground is shaking under our feet and the leaves make it hard to keep our balance but he's scrambling towards me.

"Jonny!" I scream and just barely manage to catch his hand before we both fall to the ground. It's hard not to roll but I dig my heels into the dirt and manage to keep myself from slipping further.

It's like the world is splitting apart. The creature is being woven together with thick branches and propped up with tree trunks. The groaning of the wood is now a chorus of screams that rip through the air. I can just barely see the priest through the thick fog.

"Spirit! I command you to leave this holy place! You are the devil placed on this earth to harm good people!" He shouts. The creature is finally fully formed with its eyes glowing through the fog. Sharp, twisted branches shoot out of its body, and a mouth full of splintered wood drops open as it lets out another shriek. It looks at all of us, one by one, and then focuses on the priest.

"You must leave! Leave in the name of the Lord!" The priest raises the hand holding the Bible. The creature turns to stare before a branch shoots out from its body. Before I can even see what has happened, the priest's body falls to the ground and blood is pooling on the forest floor. The creature turns to stare at all of us again and takes a step forward. Its body is looming over the ruins of the house.

"Oh my God." I gasp. The world is bending in alarming ways and I feel like I'm about to start falling up into the sky when I see Jaci and Naja standing on the ground, steady on their feet.

"Spirit." Jaci nods to the creature. "I am Jaci."

The moment he speaks, the world rights itself. I'm still lying on the ground but I can feel gravity pulling me towards the ground. I can feel Jonny's arms wrapped around me tightly and we're both gasping as we both watch this showdown.

"I am Naja." Naja nods. The two siblings step closer together, holding hands. The creature seems to be panting and leaves are fluttering down around it and I can hear the rustling of the leaves. Its glowing eyes are fixated on the two siblings as they walk closer.

"We are people from this land. We are the bloodline of this soil." Naja says. The creature stops panting. They step closer.

"We see you. And we see your pain. We see your anger." Jaci says. The branch that impaled the priest through the throat buries itself into the ground, leaving only a small hole near the priest's still body. They step closer again.

"But this is not the way to go about this," Naja says. The thorny spines that were poking out through the creature's woven shell retract, leaving only a woven pattern to make up its body. They step closer again.

"There are people here now, people who live here," Jaci explains. It seems to pain all three of them when he says that and they all exchange sad looks. The branches that make up the creature's face twist up with pain. They step closer.

"Just the same as you once did," Naja says. The creature's mouth opens again but this time, instead of a scream, it's a soft whimper. Not in one voice but the voices of many, all heavy with sorrow. The creaking wood starts to sound like creaking bones. They step closer again.

"Times have changed," Jaci says. The creature lowers itself to the ground and Jaci places a hand on its body. Small branches snake up his arm, almost like it's holding his hand,

"You need to leave," Naja says, placing her hand next to her brothers. The creature rests itself on the ground before the two of them pull their hands away and move to the body of the priest. They're careful to avoid touching him, but they pick up the Bible and hold it open for the creature to inspect.

It reaches over and seems to inspect the book for a moment before its glowing eyes shut and the trees that made up its body fall apart, crushing the last traces of the ruins. The sound only lasts a second as a dozen trees come crashing down and Jonny throws himself over me. Pieces of wood and branches pelt us but it's over in just a moment.

"Is it over?" I ask after a moment of silence. Jonny gets off of me and we get to our feet unsteadily. Everyone stands up to see Jaci and Naja toss the Bible into the fire.

"It is," Naja says, her eyes fixed on the fire as it licked up at the Bible and then burst into flames. "The spirit is gone. They are quiet."

Annie's father walks over to all of us again with Annie still in his arms. He looks absolutely shocked but after a moment of protest, he places Annie back on the ground. She wanders over to Jaci and Naja, holding their eyes for a moment before leaning in to give them both a hug.

"Is he dead?" Annie asks, noticing the body on the ground for the first time. She's surprisingly calm about it but Jaci and Naja glance to study the body for a moment.

"Oh, almost certainly," Naja says. The body is drained white and the pool of blood around his body is soaking into his black robes. "There is no spirit in him anymore. And it was a bad spirit to begin with."

I stare at the priest's body. Something is unsettling about the stillness but at this point, the exhaustion of this day is settling into my body and Jonny is keeping me on my feet.

"What do we do now?" I ask. We all look around at each other. Jonny, Annie, her father, Jaci, and Naja. We're the only ones who witnessed what happened in the woods today. We're the only ones who know what happened to all of those missing people. My knees give out and Jonny gasps, moving to hold me up. My arms wrap around him as he slowly lowers me to the ground.

"I think we should call the police," Annie says.

And the world goes black.

Chapter 11

"How are you feeling today?" Jonny asks. We're taking a slow walk outside and the summer wind is starting to get a bit cooler. Soon, it'll be fall and school will start up again. The doctors say that I should make a full recovery by then. Still, Jonny sticks close to me and his arm is wrapped protectively around me as we walk around at a slow pace.

"Better. You don't have to worry about me, I'm fine now." I roll my eyes. I spent a good week or so in the hospital, unconscious. That one day, with all of its stress and chaos, took a toll on my body. Jonny, Annie, and my mother stuck by my side nearly the entire time. It's been two weeks since that, though, and I'm starting to get stronger again.

"I know," Jonny says. I know that he had a particularly hard time while I was unconscious. He slept in the hospital room, according to my mom. They became fast friends during that week and now he has a key to the house to visit whenever he wants.

And he visits nearly every day. It's been the best thing for my recovery, more than anything else the doctors could give me.

"So... what's been going on?" I ask. Jonny thinks for a moment. He's been my connection with the news surrounding the summer camp, along with Annie. They're the ones that know what really happened there and Jonny starts to tell me this week's news.

"Annie's father has been trying to sort things out with the police. It's not a lot of fun so she's been hanging out at my place a lot. It's a really difficult thing to explain, especially since he can't really tell them that the ghosts of a bunch of dead people killed the priest." Jonny says. We both stay in silence for a little while, trying to fight back memories of that day. It isn't an easy thing to forget, though. "They found those populars."

That catches my attention. I search Jonny's face but his expression is cold and angry. I can tell that he still hasn't gotten past what those boys did to us.

"The ones that chased us?" I ask, trying to prompt a response out of him. He nods.

"Yeah. And a few of the people who went missing." He pauses like he's trying to figure out what to say next. I know that he and Annie sometimes keep the news away from me to make sure that I don't stress out about it. I don't know how to feel about it. Sometimes it's irritating, sometimes I'm thankful for it. Hearing news about what happened sometimes makes me have nightmares for days and I have to take the sleeping pills they prescribed me.

"They just... turned up?" I ask. I'm feeling a bit better today and a bit braver, too. Jonny glances at me, looking me up and down and seems to make up his mind.

"They're dead. But it seems like their bodies have turned up. All fresh, too, even the people who went missing weeks ago." He says. His eyes don't leave mine and I know he's watching for a reaction.

My stomach twists up into knots. It's not an easy thing to hear, even about people who were as awful as they were. But it's happened and there's nothing I can do about it now.

"And what else?" I prod again. I want to hear about everything, I want to be up to date on everything that has happened. Jonny seems to hear that in my voice and nods.

"Summer camp's being shut down. A lot of lawsuits for kids going missing, hate crimes, lack of safety." He says.

"Oh, that's awful!" I know that summer camp was special for Annie and Jonny. That's how they met and Annie told me that going actually helped him out a lot. Jonny only shrugs though.

"Nah. It was bound to happen eventually, even without all of this." He says with a smile. I remember all of the ridiculous stories about summer camp that he told me when I was still bedridden and smile. He's probably right. It's a miracle that it stayed open this long.

"So what's happening to it? The camp?" I ask.

"They're selling the land to some developer or something. Apparently, they're building a mall there soon." He says. It's not the most interesting thing and we continue to walk. We're getting to a nicer part of my neighborhood and I lead him down the sidewalk to my childhood playground. It's still standing, looking a little worse for wear, but Jonny opens up the chained-up door for me with a bobby pin.

It takes a little while and Jonny has to help me but I manage to climb up the little obstacle courses until we're both sitting on a bridge between two towers. Our legs dangle off the edge and we stare off to the mountains where the camp used to be. The sun is just starting to set and the air cools even more. It's soothing.

"How are you?" I ask after our moment of silence. Jonny turns to look at me, looking a little surprised.

"Me?" He asks. I laugh, shaking my head.

"Yeah. We both went through that together, are you okay?"

There's a moment of silence. In the last two weeks, it seems like Jonny's been taking care of me 24/7. Honestly, he has. The first week after I woke up, he didn't leave the room for more than ten minutes and he was right there with my mom in taking care of me, even when I got back home. Half of the time, when I woke from a nightmare, he would be the one to calm me down.

"It was super weird." He whispers. I know that he's thinking of camp. The memories are foggy for me now but I know it's different for him. He and Annie talk about it a lot and he's been questioned by the police now. It's not an easy thing and I can see it weighing on him.

"Yeah." I agree, waiting for him to say more. He doesn't and I drop it. If he wants to talk about it, he will, in his own time. Instead, he reached out to take my hand and squeezed it. It's become our little thing, even before I was in the hospital. I smile, looking down at our linked hands.

"What are we?" He finally asks. It takes me a moment to realize what he's said and then I burst into laughter.

"Is that really what you're thinking of? What we are? After everything that we've survived?" I ask, squeezing his hand. Jonny's face breaks into a smile and we're both laughing, my head pressed against his shoulder.

"Well... yeah!" He shrugs and we're laughing again. I can't believe that's the thing that's been bothering him. After being questioned by the police, taking care of me in a coma, and watching everything unfurl... he's been thinking of that. "I don't know, I just... I was thinking about it a lot."

I stop laughing. I can't say that I haven't been thinking about it, too, but with everything that's been going on, it never felt like the right time to talk to him about what we had between us.

"I don't know. What do you want us to be?" I ask. He looks at me, shakes his head, and then stares off to the mountains again.

"I'm no good at this kind of stuff." He sighs. I squeeze his hand and give him a moment. I've gotten to know Jonny. He's surprisingly shy, considering everything, and he struggles with putting his feelings into words sometimes. He just needs some time sometimes.

"Romance. That kind of stuff. I'm..." He trails off.

"You're used to getting into trouble." I offer. He smiles, turning back to me. I know that I'm right when I see the little shine in his eyes.

"Yeah. And you're not really trouble. I don't know, being around you is really good for me. Annie's noticed it, too, and even though it gets stressful sometimes I just feel... I don't know, I just want to take care of you. And I don't really want to do all that crazy stuff anymore." He rambles. His hand is clinging onto mine and he looks up at me. There's the shine of tears in his eyes and a shake in his voice as he shrugs a little with a smile on his face. "It's actually kind of nice."

I can't help leaning in to kiss him. I want to be closer to him and I take a deep breath. The smell of cigarettes, the woods, his cologne. It's a smell that I've come to love. His mouth moves against mine and his free hand is cupping my face, gently pulling me closer.

It's the first kiss we've shared since that first night together. It's just as thrilling and my heart is hammering in my heart, even when we finally break apart.

"So... what are we?" I ask again, trying to catch my breath. I don't know if it's because of the kiss or because I'm just tired from all the walking today but I barely care. I'm staring up at Jonny, waiting for his answer.

"Boyfriends?" He finally offers. I feel myself melt against him, my head on his shoulder. The night air is finally starting to set in and we watch the sun set.

"That sounds nice."

Epilogue

There's a knock on my bedroom door and I glance up for a moment, confused. My mom isn't supposed to be home for another couple of hours but the door opens up before I can question it.

Jonny steps in with a big smile already on his face. His hair is grown out enough for it to be tied up into a long, curly ponytail. He's wearing a black tank top with black jeans, even in this weather. I don't mind at all, though. It shows off his muscular arms and I can't help but stare at him. His usually pale skin has a healthy glow to it now.

He's so similar yet different to the boy I met last year at summer camp. It was a strange way to start our relationship but it certainly was memorable. Since then, we've been dating and we're getting close to our first anniversary.

"Hey, babe," Jonny says, walking over to my bed and leaning over me to press a kiss to my forehead.

"Oh, hey!" I roll over onto my back, giving him room on the bed to join me. He kicks off of his boots and cuddles up next to me, wrapping his arms around me and hugging me close. "How are you?"

"Doing well. I just finished up my summer class." He sighs. He's been trying to do well in school and in just one school year, he managed to pull enough passing grades to graduate, even though he was two years behind just last summer.

"Good. Proud of you." I turn to him, pushing back his hair and pressing a kiss to his cheek.

"Thanks, babe." He glances at the papers and books open on my bed that I was working on just a moment ago. His eyes scan over it quickly and I can see the curiosity in his face. "And what about you?"

"Working on- ah!" I begin to say before I feel his lips press to my neck and bite teasingly. I don't even get a chance before his hands are reaching up under my shirt and holding me close to him again. His hips roll against me and I gasp.

"Come on. Let's take a break." He mutters into my ear. I can't help but the flush that comes to my face and I groan.

"God, Jonny." I gasp. My hands are on him as he makes quick work of both of our clothes. His hands reach up my shirt and tossing it aside before he tugs off my sweatpants.

I get to have a good look at him when he gets onto his knees and tugs off his tank top. I've seen it dozens of times before but I still can't help but adore his body. His body is sculpted and muscular and familiar to me now.

"You're cute." He mutters into my ear. He presses a kiss to my neck and then my collarbone and my stomach, teasing me. It's hard to bite back on my moans but he's making me gasp and shaking in minutes. "Really cute."

He tosses aside his own pants and we're both naked. He looks up at me with a glint in his eyes before he presses down on me and we both gasp.

"Fuck." He mutters through gritted teeth as he buries his face in my shoulder. I can do little more than wrap my arms around him and whimper into his ear as he furiously chases his orgasm. The feeling of him rubbing against me, our members pressed together and stroking each other is an absolutely intoxicating feeling.

"Jonny!" I moan as he thrusts hard against me and with a shuddering breath, Jonny's trembling all over and I feel the warm splatters land on my stomach. I have to bite back on my own whining moans as I wait for him to finish.

"Fucking Christ. That was great." Jonny breathes before he props himself up on his knees. He seems to be admiring his seed on my body before he realizes that my face is still twisted up in frustration. "Did you not finish?"

"Nope. Want to help?" I ask but it sounds more like I'm begging him. He smirks, taking his hand retying his hair into a ponytail before scooting himself down on the bed and looking up at me from in between my legs.

"Absolutely." He leans down and I can feel his hot breath against my twitching member. I'm too close for him to really tease me too much but he lingers there for a few moments before I thrust my hips up towards his mouth.

"God, you're so fucking pretty." He says finally before he opens his mouth and slowly takes me into his mouth. The tightness, the hot wetness is almost immediately overwhelming. His head is bobbing and I watch as my shaft disappears into his mouth and go lightheaded at the sight of it. It's not long before Jonny has to have his hands on my hips, pinning me down against the mattress as I squirm and spill into his mouth.

It takes me a minute to recover but by then Jonny's got me cleaned up and we're cuddled up against each other. As always, his muscular arms are wrapped around me and his hands are playing with my hair.

"I love you."

"I love you, too."